Folk Fashion

North American Folklore

Children's Folklore

Christmas and Santa Claus Folklore

Contemporary Folklore

Ethnic Folklore

Family Folklore

Firefighters' Folklore

Folk Arts and Crafts

Folk Customs

Folk Dance

Folk Fashion

Folk Festivals

Folk Games

Folk Medicine

Folk Music

Folk Proverbs and Riddles

Folk Religion

Folk Songs

Folk Speech

Folk Tales and Legends

Food Folklore

Regional Folklore

North American Folklore

Folk Fashion

BY SHERRY BONNICE

Mason Crest Publishers

Mason Crest Publishers Inc.
370 Reed Road
Broomall, Pennsylvania 19008
(866) MCP-BOOK (toll free)
www.masoncrest.com

First printing
1 2 3 4 5 6 7 8 9 10
Library of Congress Cataloging-in-Publication Data on file at the Library of Congress.
ISBN 1-59084-338-X
        1-59084-328-2 (series)

Design by Lori Holland.
Composition by Bytheway Publishing Services, Binghamton, New York.
Cover design by Joe Gilmore.
Printed and bound in the Hashemite Kingdom of Jordan.

Picture credits:
Corbis: pp. 18, 39, 61, 70, 80
Corel: pp. 6, 11, 13, 20, 41, 56, 60, 62, 63, 68, 72, 75, 77, 87, 97
Eclectic Collections: p. 73
J. Rowe: pp. 8, 22, 25, 34, 36, 48, 50, 58, 92, 94
Photo Alto: pp. 32, 43,
Photo Disc: pp. 30, 51, 53, 74, 82, 84, 85, 86, 96, 100
Cover: "Choosing a Bonnet" by Norman Rockwell © 1931 SEPS: Licensed by Curtis
        Publishing, Indianapolis, IN. www.curtispublishing.com

Printed by permission of the Norman Rockwell Family
© the Norman Rockwell Family Entities

Contents

Folklore grows from long-ago
seeds. Just as an acorn sends
down roots even as it shoots
up leaves across the sky,
folklore is rooted deeply in the
past and yet still lives and
grows today. It spreads
through our modern world
with branches as wide and
sturdy as any oak's;
it grounds us in yesterday
even as it helps us make
sense of both the present and
the future.

Introduction

by Dr. Alan Jabbour

WHAT DO A TALE, a joke, a fiddle tune, a quilt, a jig, a game of jacks, a saint's day procession, a snake fence, and a Halloween costume have in common? Not much, at first glance, but all these forms of human creativity are part of a zone of our cultural life and experience that we sometimes call "folklore."

The word "folklore" means the cultural traditions that are learned and passed along by ordinary people as part of the fabric of their lives and culture. Folklore may be passed along in verbal form, like the urban legend that we hear about from friends who assure us that it really happened to a friend of their cousin. Or it may be tunes or dance steps we pick up on the block, or ways of shaping things to use or admire out of materials readily available to us, like that quilt our aunt made. Often we acquire folklore without even fully realizing where or how we learned it.

Though we might imagine that the word "folklore" refers to cultural traditions from far away or long ago, we actually use and enjoy folklore as part of our own daily lives. It is often ordinary, yet we often remember and prize it because it seems somehow very special. Folklore is culture we share with others in our communities, and we build our identities through the sharing. Our first shared identity is family identity, and family folklore such as shared meals or prayers or songs helps us develop a sense of belonging. But as we grow older we learn to belong to other groups as well. Our identities may be ethnic, religious, occupational, or regional—or all of these, since no one has only one cultural identity. But in every case, the identity is anchored and strengthened by a variety of cultural traditions in which we participate and share with our neighbors. We feel the threads of connection with people we know, but the threads extend far beyond our own immediate communities. In a real sense, they connect us in one way or another to the world.

Folklore possesses features by which we distinguish ourselves from each other. A certain dance step may be African American, or a certain story urban, or a certain hymn Protestant, or a certain food preparation Cajun. Folklore can distinguish us, but at the same time it is one of the best ways we introduce ourselves to each other. We learn about new ethnic groups on the North American landscape by sampling their cuisine, and we enthusiastically adopt musical ideas from other communities. Stories, songs, and visual designs move from group to group, enriching all people in the process. Folklore thus is both a sign of identity, experienced as a special marker of our special groups, and at the same time a cultural coin that is well spent by sharing with others beyond our group boundaries.

Folklore is usually learned informally. Somebody, somewhere, taught us that jump rope rhyme we know, but we may have trouble remembering just where we got it, and it probably wasn't in a book that was assigned as homework. Our world has a domain of formal knowledge, but folklore is a domain of knowledge and culture that is learned by sharing and imitation rather than formal instruction. We can study it formally—that's what we are doing now!—but its natural arena is in the informal, person-to-person fabric of our lives.

Not all culture is folklore. Classical music, art sculpture, or great novels are forms of high art that may contain folklore but are not themselves folklore. Popular music or art may be built on folklore themes and traditions, but it addresses a much wider and more diverse audience than folk music or folk art. But even in the world of popular and mass culture, folklore keeps popping up around the margins. E-mail is not folklore—but an e-mail smile is. And college football is not folklore—but the wave we do at the stadium is.

This series of volumes explores the many faces of folklore throughout the North American continent. By illuminating the many aspects of folklore in our lives, we hope to help readers of the series to appreciate more fully the richness of the cultural fabric they either possess already or can easily encounter as they interact with their North American neighbors.

People have always used clothes to define their identities, to reflect back to themselves and to the rest of the world their concepts of who they are.

ONE

Fashion and Identity
Clothes That Tell Who We Are

Some of us have had nightmares where we're going about our business, only to discover that, like the poor emperor, we're naked. The fear of being exposed in all our naked foolishness is common to us all.

ONCE THERE WAS an emperor who loved himself. He loved his castle and his furnishings, he loved his courtyard and his throne, but he especially loved his clothes. Every day he ordered his servants to prepare a parade so he could show off his royal garments. As he paraded through the streets, everyone admired him. The emperor was very proud of his appearance.

The royal seamstresses were kept busy morning and night, designing and making new outfits for the emperor. Then one fine day two strangers appeared at the royal palace asking for an audience with his highness. The royal ministers told them that the emperor was occupied with official business and would not see anyone. In truth he was being fitted for his newest outfit, and his ministers knew he was never to be bothered during this time.

"But we are the very finest weavers in the kingdom. Our cloth is made from exquisite gold and silver thread. Our fabric is so amazing," they said, "that it is invisible to anyone who is foolish and empty-headed."

When the emperor heard of this wonderful fabric, he knew he had to have some for himself. With it he would not only have the most beautiful clothes in the kingdom but he would also be able to keep only the most competent people in his palace. Those who could not see the cloth would be banished from his service.

The emperor ordered the ministers to bring the strangers to the throne room.

"What do you need to make this beautiful cloth?" the emperor asked them.

"We need a large loom and shuttles. The finest gold and silver thread must also be bought. And we need lots of food because it takes a great deal of energy to work on a project such as this one," said the first stranger.

"And we need a great sum of money because we are the finest weavers in the kingdom," said the second stranger.

Everything was brought to a large, comfortable room. The emperor's servants provided the strangers with all their needs as they pretended to work. The loom was empty and the threads had been hidden in a trunk.

The emperor heard the loom working morning, noon, and sometimes far into the night. He was very anxious to see the cloth but was afraid to be the first to view it. He sent his prime minister, who saw nothing when he looked at the loom. The minister wondered if he was empty-headed. In fear he said, "This is the most wonderful cloth. Yes, yes, it is."

The emperor was happy to hear the minister's thoughts. About a week later the emperor sent the assistant minister, who hurried to the loom to look at the cloth. He saw nothing also. *Oh, no,* he thought. *If I am foolish, I will lose my job.* He also told the emperor of the fabric's beautiful design.

Soon the outfit was complete. The ministers planned a most wonderful procession, and the

> It is an interesting question how far men would retain their relative rank if they were divested of their clothes.
> —*Henry David Thoreau*

Today fashion is not only important to us as individuals; it has also become a business in its own right. While fashion shows like this one may help to shape clothing trends, however, our choices about what we wear still reflect both our cultural heritage and our individuality.

royal subjects filled the streets, waiting to see the emperor in his new clothes. When the strangers showed the emperor his imaginary outfit, he was stunned. He could not see his new clothes. Was he, the emperor, empty-headed? It could not be so.

The emperor put on the make-believe clothes. He pretended he loved them. The ministers agreed with him that he looked quite handsome, and the procession began. But the emperor's subjects looked at him in astonishment. They did not want to seem foolish, but no one could see the emperor's new clothes.

Finally a small child called from the crowd, "The emperor is naked."

Everyone agreed. But the foolish emperor held his head high and continued the procession back to the palace.

WHAT we wear tells a lot about us. The fabrics we choose, the colors, and the styles all add details to our clothing tale. Just like the emperor, we want others to like how we look, and our appearance reinforces our self-esteem. Sometimes we want to look different from others so those who see us question what is important to us. Or we simply dress for comfort while we work, play, or relax. Whatever our motivations, how we dress sends a message to those with whom we interact. We tell them something about ourselves—and when we view their clothing we learn something about them.

Years ago many people did not have the choices we have today. Most only had the materials available in the area where they lived. Others were forced by their social status to wear certain articles of clothing and not others. In ancient Rome, for instance, slaves wore tunics while a toga worn over a tunic indicated Roman citizenship. The togas of **magistrates** were decorated with purple bands.

Folk fashion includes the traditional dress and tales of clothing shared from generation to generation. In European countries, costumes varied from village to village. Many people did not

> To be out of fashion is more criminal than to be seen in a state of nature.
> —*Abigail Adams*

The toga was the proper attire for the well-dressed Roman.

We can tell these people's jobs just by looking at their clothing.

travel far from home, and changing fashion influences were not a part of their culture. For this reason ancient garments changed slowly.

Today, ancestral folk costumes are usually worn on special occasions or to commemorate holidays. Some may be the same garments worn by a parent or grandparent kept safely tucked away for years anticipating a new generation. The oldest daughter whose ancestors moved to America from Sweden might wear a long, white dress and a wreath in her hair with candles to commemorate St. Lucia Day. Dressed in this traditional costume, she shares coffee and treats with her family and friends.

Another young girl with a Scottish heritage might plan a wedding in which she wears a traditional white gown but the groom and her father wear their highland dress, including kilts, vests, and bow ties. The Scottish tradition of tartan kilts and vests made with the plaids of the family name expresses both their cultural heritage and their family identity. The wearers are proud of their Scottish ancestry.

Historians have found that dressing in fashion has been going on for a long time. Oddly enough, usually the more powerful and rich people were, the more uncomfortable their

STYLES THAT HURT

During the 1840s and 1850s women's skirts reached such voluminous proportions that the skirts' total weight might be 15 to 20 pounds. Women wore at least two layers of petticoats and sometimes up to six were required for evening wear. Carrying around so much weight was hard enough, but corsets worn at the same time were laced as tightly as possible. Some squeezed a woman's ribs so she could barely move, and internal organs were sometimes pushed out of place. Walking or sitting was difficult, and bending was almost impossible. When fashions changed in the 1880s, however, bustles, tight bodices, narrow sleeves, and long trains became stylish—and these were equally restrictive.

Full skirts and corseted waists limited a woman's ability to move, let alone breathe.

Sweat suits are appropriate for exercise—but today they are equally appropriate for a trip to the mall.

clothing. Meanwhile, those who worked needed to be able to move freely to accomplish their jobs, so they wore clothes without any restrictions.

Without a doubt, clothes play an important role in our lives. Just as the vain emperor was persuaded to invest in clothes that would be **aesthetically** pleasing, as well as give him power over those who viewed them, many believe that the right apparel can give us power in certain situations. On our first date we want to wear the perfect outfit; if we are interviewing for a job we agonize over what to wear; and special holidays are more memorable when we dress in something festive.

Unlike other folk customs that remain in families or within groups for years, however, fashion changes may keep us from realizing the traditions expressed by our clothes.

For instance, our everyday clothing many times identifies the jobs we perform. When we see a man in a uniform, we at once recognize his profession. He may be a police officer, fireman, or possibly a member of the armed forces. In most cases, the cloth

In China, the upper classes once bound women's feet; these women could barely walk on their tiny, deformed feet, but their helplessness and uselessness were seen as reflections of their family's wealth and prestige rather than as handicaps. Europeans found this custom barbaric—but for centuries, European women wore elaborate and uncomfortable clothes that limited the amount and kinds of work they could accomplish. This was a way to prove their husband's position and prosperity. This clothing tradition was not so very different from the Chinese foot binding custom.

and style of his clothes have been updated, but his uniform is still a traditional garment worn for as long as that service has existed.

Not long ago if you saw someone in sweat pants and running shoes, you would assume he had just completed or was about to engage in some form of exercise. But in this case, styles have relaxed in recent years, and this outfit has become merely a form of casual dress for young and old, male and female.

Although the primary reason we wear clothes is for protection and warmth, the style of clothes we choose is a declaration of our personality. We sometimes dress for practical reasons, which in many cases is how we dress when we are at home. We also dress to make an impression or to look as we believe others expect. Sometimes our dress is similar whether we dress casually or "dress-up."

In the following chapters we will look at different styles of clothing and the reasons people choose to dress the way they do. For some it is a matter of being "like" everyone else. For others a choice to *dress* differently means a decision to *act* differently also. Distinct clothing can be an outward show of what is unique about people spiritually or socially. Others dress in certain ways because economically they have no choice, while some wear what is most fitting for their occupation.

As the years went by, skirts became smaller—but an unnatural, wasp-like waist was still the fashion. Only brutally tight corsets could create such a shape.

Whenever we get dressed, we reveal something about our age, our social background, our personality, and sometimes even our mood. Think about what you have on right now. What are your clothes communicating to others about you? Each time we choose which clothes to wear, we are influenced by many factors. The foolish emperor cared most about impressing others and gaining power over them. What motivated you this morning when you got dressed?

Today many people like to connect with the traditions of the past by dressing up in old-fashioned clothes. Tourists enjoy visiting places where they can get a glimpse of the way their great-great-grandparents dressed and lived.

TWO

The Customs
We Wear
Costume and Tradition

Contemporary Native Americans affirm their cultural identity by wearing the traditional costumes of their people. The bright feathers and lavishly beaded accessories proclaim to the world who these men are.

INTERESTINGLY ENOUGH, the words *custom* and *costume* both come from the same Latin roots. That original word had to do with self and identity, with the habits a person used for self-expression. Custom and clothing both affirm individual identity—and yet both are shared from generation to generation. In every country, customs keep families connected to their past and their future—and costumes were created as a result of the customs of a given people. Because most customs often have special occasions as their focal points, costumes for such occasions also became a popular part of a family's history.

North America is very young historically. Many traditions observed today were brought with settlers as they moved away from their homelands. Colonists crossed the ocean for different reasons, including religious persecution, wealth, and the desire for a new adventurous life. Whatever the settlers' reasons and from wherever they came, most brought the traditional clothing of their homelands with them. Old customs—and costumes—remained rooted in the past, even as they were transformed by the new environment.

ONCE there was a girl who was very lazy. Her mother was poor and needed her help with spinning thread to make their clothes—but the daughter was always wandering off, neglecting the constant spinning. One day, as the mother was punishing her daughter for her laziness, a prince, Lord of the Red Castle, saw her.

"Why do you punish the girl?" he asked.

Today we think of spinning as a fairy-tale occupation. But two hundred years ago, spinning was an ongoing chore for many young women.

"She is lazy and does nothing but spin **hemp** into gold," her mother answered. She did not mean her daughter could really perform such a miracle; she only meant the girl was a daydreamer who expected that work could do itself, money would grow on trees . . . and hemp could be spun into gold. But the prince misunderstood.

"If she can spin hemp into gold," he cried, "I will purchase her from you."

The mother was so desperate and so frustrated she sold her daughter. The poor girl was

> Folktales often give us a glimpse into a culture's hopes, dreams, and fears. In the story of Kinkach Martinko, we can see an earlier society's everyday frustrations and fantasies.

Folktales often spread from country to country, the same story popping up in various languages around the world. In the German version of Kinkach Martinko, the little man's name was Rumpelstiltskin.

taken to the prince's castle and locked in a room filled with hemp, a **distaff**, and a spinning wheel.

"When you finish spinning this hemp into gold I will marry you," the prince said as he left.

The girl cried and cried. Suddenly, though, she saw an odd-looking man sitting on the windowsill. He was dressed in a red cap and wore boots made from a strange material.

"Why are you so unhappy?" he asked.

"I must spin all this hemp into gold and I cannot do it."

"I will do it for you. It will take me three days. If you cannot guess my name and tell me what my boots are made of, at the end of that time you will be mine."

The poor girl answered yes without thinking.

The little man laughed and began spinning. He worked all day long. Finally he asked the girl if she knew his name or what his boots were made from.

"No," she replied.

He laughed again and disappeared through the window.

The girl thought and thought about his name and his boots. She was so involved in her problem that she forgot to eat her dinner. When she heard cries from outside, she looked out the window and saw an old man sitting beside the castle wall.

"Why are you upset?" the girl asked him.

"I am going to die of thirst and hunger," he said.

Without hesitating, the girl gave him her dinner. They talked for a short time, and she told him to come back the next day.

In the morning the little man arrived and began spinning. Once again he worked all day spinning the hemp into gold thread. And once again he asked the girl his name and if she knew what his boots were made from. And again she answered no.

That night as the girl gave her dinner to the old man, her eyes were filled with tears. She knew she would never guess the spinner's name, nor the stuff his boots were made from, unless a miracle happened.

"Why are you so sad?" the old man asked her.

For a long time she would not answer, but at last she told him her problem.

He listened intently and then said, "Today as I came through the woods I saw a little man in a red hat jumping over nine pots he had placed around a burning wood pile. He sang this song as he went:

> *My sweet friend, the fair maiden, at the Red Castle near,*
> *Two days and two nights seeks my name to divine,*
> *She'll never find out, so the third night 'tis clear*
> *My sweet friend, the fair maiden, can't fail to be mine.*
> *Hurrah! for my name is Kinkach Martinko,*
> *Hurrah! for my boots are of dog's skin O!"*

"That's what you need to know, my dear girl," the old man told her. "So do not forget and you are saved." And with these words the old man vanished.

The next morning the little man appeared again and worked throughout the day. When he was finished he looked at the girl and smiled with confidence. He demanded she tell him the answers.

"Your name is Kinkach Martinko, and your boots are made of dog skin," she replied without the slightest hesitation.

When he heard the words, he spun around on the floor like a top, tore out his hair, and beat his breast with rage. And then he rushed out of the window like a whirlwind.

The girl was grateful for the old man's help, but he never returned so she could thank him. The prince married her as he had promised, and she was very happy as a princess. What's more, she had such a good stock of gold thread that she never had to spin again for the rest of her life.

TODAY most of us buy our clothes at the mall or department store—but for our ancestors, the production of clothing was a long and hard process. The creation of a simple woolen garment meant raising and caring for sheep, shearing the wool, cleaning it and preparing it for spinning, spinning it into thread, weaving or knitting it into fabric, and then sewing it into a garment. Similar steps were involved in the production of linen, silk, or cotton—except each of these fabrics came from a different natural source. As a result, clothing was valuable (as treasured as the gold spun by Kinkach Martinko), and only the wealthy could afford

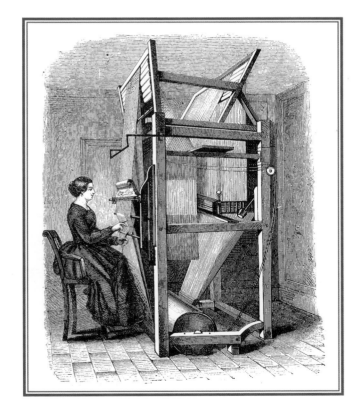

Weaving was considered "women's work." Large looms like these made their jobs easier, but creating a piece of cloth was still a long process.

to own very many clothes. Ordinary people worked hard for each piece of clothing they wore.

Men might raise the animals or grow the crops that produced fibers for fabric—but women like the poor lazy girl in this Polish folktale were the ones who transformed the fiber into clothing. Unless she was wealthy, a good part of a woman's life would be spent making clothes; no wonder then if young women sometimes rebelled against the constant labor. Today an adolescent girl might daydream about an unlimited shopping spree at her favorite clothing store—but girls from earlier cultures probably dreamed of being transformed into princesses who would never have to spin and weave again. Spinning thread continued to be a familiar and time-consuming job for most of the women who settled North America. The Polish folktale of Kinkach Martinko was rooted in the Old World—but it still made sense to New World settlers.

Many Polish people immigrated to America in its early days, including the Polish Count Casimir Pulaski, who gave his life in the Revolutionary War's fight for freedom. Like others coming to the new land, Poles brought their customs and costumes with them. Polish folk costumes were made with fabrics created and decorated by the local people. Most of the clothing was produced from linen, cotton, wool, felt, leather, and fur available in the community. The peasant folk had to make do with whatever natural fibers were at hand.

Many people wore their costumes daily. Two versions of the costume were made, however; one from rougher cloth was worn to work while

> Even women in the most remote places kept a separate garment for special occasions. Sometimes it might be just a pretty shawl to cover an everyday dress. Then as today, when women wanted to celebrate, they needed something to wear.

> Linen comes from the flax plant; silk comes from the fiber spun by the silkworm; and cotton comes from the cotton plant.

more elaborate dress was reserved for special occasions. These special occasion dresses, vests, and skirts were often very skillfully made and usually highly ornamented. Polish women understandably were proud of their stitching skills and sometimes spent months sewing elaborate embroidery on their clothing.

Besides being distinctive from country to country, clothing that was brought to North America was often distinctive from village to village. The Krakow costume, named for the town in Poland where it originated, is one well-known costume. Men's pants were striped with red and white. The metallic ringlets attached to the belt were from the armor of ancient times. The sleeveless coat with military type tassels was called a *kabat* and was originally fashionable during the time of Napoleon. A four-cornered red hat called *rogatywka* was decorated with ribbons and peacock feathers. The woman's costume included a beautifully embroidered and beaded velvet vest and floral **challis** skirt. If the wearer was single, she donned a wreath of flowers in her hair; if married she wore a white kerchief.

As the years went by, outside influences affected most clothing choices. Economic stand-

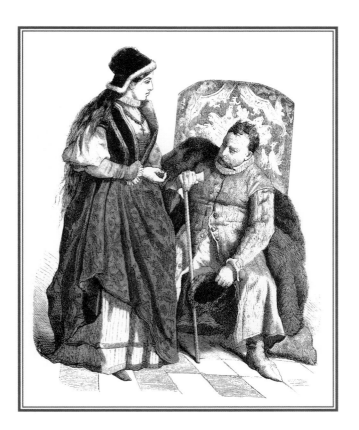

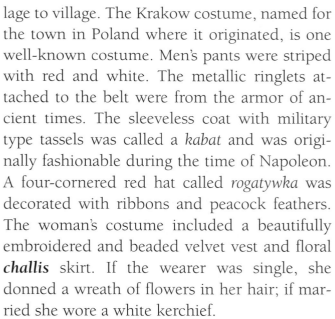

Traditional Polish clothing.

ing provided the means to acquire clothing or cloth to make garments. Much of the population had limited means to buy clothes. For average people, growing crops or raising sheep provided the raw materials, which were then spun into cloth. Because it was not easily replaced, clothing in the early American colonies continued to be valuable.

Producing clothing may have meant long hours of toil for women, but the costumes of the settlers, as with other cultures' dress, also reflected a woman's artistry. Spinning, dying, weaving, and sewing gave her an opportunity for artistic self-expression. When

> In your clothes avoid too much gaudiness; do not value yourself upon an embroidered gown; and remember that a reasonable word, or an obliging look, will gain you more respect than all your fine trappings.
> —*George Savile*

When the sewing machine was first invented, it was a luxury few North American women could afford.

Folk costumes like these were once worn by ordinary people for "dress up" occasions.

her family looked their best in public, her own industry and skills were affirmed.

Responsible for all their families' clothing needs, women borrowed bits of current fashion trends from the more prominent women in their communities. Embellishments reflected the talent and beliefs of these seamstresses. For instance, dying threads in bright colors was one way a woman could add beauty to a garment.

Meanwhile, most clothes of the native North Americans were made from available natural resources. For instance, in the Northeast, whenever a man killed a deer for food, the family was also provided with hide for clothes. Native Americans living along the Atlantic coast made their clothes from deer hide as well as woven plant fibers. Their winter dress included thick fur robes made from otter, beaver, and bear skins. Clothing was decorated with fringe, shells, and stones, expressing the community's closeness to nature. When clothing was embellished, most of its **motifs** honored nature; animals, plants, and the earth were often depicted. Clearly, Native Americans' relationship to nature affected their clothing, demonstrating once again the close connection between custom and costume.

Native Americans' clothing was hand-fash-

CLOTHING TAXES

Unmarried men were once taxed according to the worth of their wardrobes.

ioned, but wealthy white women purchased their fashions from England or France. Their clothing continued to reflect the styles of Europe—but most pioneer women, like Native Americans, made their own clothes by hand. These women created a style of clothes uniquely **indigenous** to North America. The new costumes worn daily by ordinary folk reflected the culture growing in the

She had a womanly instinct that clothes possess an influence more powerful over many than the worth of character or the magic of manners.
—*Louisa May Alcott*

Children today may dress up in folk costumes for special occasions, affirming their cultural heritage.

Feathers and animal skins were important to native fashion.

New World. Many people still kept special clothing traditions brought from their home-lands, but as the New World gained a new identity so did its people—and their clothes reflected their new customs and lifestyle.

QUILLS AND BEADS

Many Native Americans used an art form called quillwork to embellish clothes. Using mostly geometric designs, they worked with dyed porcupine or bird quills. Once glass beads became available from white traders, Indian women began replacing quills in their embroidery work with the beads that came in a wide variety of bright colors.

These Hasidic Jews proclaim their faith with the clothes they wear.

THREE

Fashion and Faith
Religious Clothing

Holiness and clothing were closely related according to Jewish traditions. For a holy man to abandon the traditional clothes required for prayer was a statement of radical and unorthodox faith.

ONCE IN A POOR Jewish village there lived a man named Zuzya. Everyone in the village brought their worries to him. One morning Zuzya was late for praying. When no one could find him they decided the only place he could be was in heaven.

There also was a stranger in the village called Stick because he was dry and lifeless. He studied night and day. When he heard that Zuzya had gone to heaven, he smiled for the first time. The thought of God and Zuzya talking to each other proved to him the ignorance of this simple community.

Stick was a curious man, so he hid under Zuzya's bed. He waited there until he could learn where Zuzya had gone instead of going to morning prayers. From his hiding place, he heard the compassionate man praying for the troubles of the people. Stick had no feeling for the people; he was full of learning instead of caring.

He watched as Zuzya got out of bed and dressed in huge boots; baggy, rough pants; a short, clumsy jacket; a big fur hat; and a long, broad leather belt studded with brass nail heads. Here was the holiest man in the village dressed like a peasant who lived in the forest. He even carried an ax in his belt as he left his house.

Stick was shocked to see the holy man dress himself in such ordinary clothing. Swallowing his horror, Stick followed Zuzya from the house into the moonlit night. He watched the holy man chop down a tree and cut the limbs into kindling. Back in the village, Zuzya walked to a poor, tumbledown shack. There he knocked,

then walked in without permission and began to light the woman's stove. She obviously assumed he was a woodcutter selling wood and insisted she could not pay him. He assured her that God, the compassionate Source of Life, would give her the six pennies that were all he asked for the wood.

As he lit the stove, Zuzya sang the morning prayers. From the window, Stick watched in surprise as the holy man ministered to this poor woman. Zuzya was not dressed for prayer—and yet Stick now realized that Zuzya was indeed holy. Zuzya taught Stick more with his actions than anything Stick had learned from all of his books.

LIKE many Jewish believers, Zuzya dressed in traditional clothing when he prayed at the **synagogue**. He was a rabbi, one of the wise men of faith who realized that what they do and how they look can make a difference to those they serve. And yet Zuzya disguised himself with ordinary clothes in order to step free of his position in the community.

For a Jew like Stick, this was a shocking and radical move. Clothing is important to traditional Jews. For them, fashion is not a question of style or whim, but a statement of faith. Halachah, the Jewish law, records the rules for how traditional Jews dress. The dress code helps identify the Jewish people to others and make them feel a part of their own community. These rules not only deal with what to wear but also how to wear it. They remind believers through everyday necessities how important it is to think about God continually.

Jews were not the only ones to connect clothing and religion.

The clothing of ancient Jewish priests was highly symbolic. Even the fringes on their clothes were not for mere decoration but to remind them of their relationship with God.

Around the time that colonists began moving to North America, a movement in Europe led believers to wear simple garments as a protest against the extravagance of the established church. Because the monarchy and wealthy members of the church dressed in the high fashion of the time, those who broke away chose to wear plain clothes as a reflection of their disapproval. Their simple clothes were also an outward sign of their inward beliefs. Like Zuzya, they chose to identify with ordinary people as a statement of their faith.

Those who left England to separate from the church were often called separatists. One of these *sects* that split from the Church of England was the Puritans. They left because they believed the church had become unethical. From reading 2 Corinthians in the Bible, they believed they were called to come away from the world and be separate. They felt the church contained rituals that were not simple and pure. Their plain life was reflected in their clothes.

The Puritans were America's Pilgrims, and today we usually imagine them wearing only black and white. Their black suits and hats have become a part of America's folklore. However,

Some Jewish clothing rules:

1. *Keep the head covered.* Men wear a skullcap called a *yarmulke* or *Kipa*. Women also wear heads covering but theirs many times reflect current fashions. This rule began as an effort by the rabbis to help people think about God. Therefore they cover their heads to remember that it is God who is above them.
2. *Wear fringes called* tzitzit *on the corners of your clothing.* The Old Testament book of Numbers 15:37 tells the people of Israel to make for themselves fringes (tzitzit) on the corners of their garments as a reminder to follow God's commandments. Because clothes used to have four corners, today traditional Jews wear a garment that is specifically made to have four corners.
3. Wear clothing from your neck to your ankles including your arms. This command is a command for modesty.
4. *Put on your right shoe first and then your left shoe. Then tie the left shoe, and finally tie the right shoe.* This may seem like a strange rule, but it is still another reminder to be mindful in each thing, to stop and think about God while doing even the most mundane chores.

wearing plain clothes did not mean Puritans wore colorless clothing. And although black, white, gray, and brown were the most common colors, documents that inventoried a person's belongings at their death listed red waistcoats, green gowns, violet cloaks, and red caps.

Once in America, Puritans adopted a less stringent dress code. They began wearing bits of lace and trim on dresses and suit coats. According to their religion's teaching, a man's financial success indicated God's approval of him and his lifestyle; consequently, those who were wealthy were eager to show their community evidence of God's approval. As with most groups, they developed a dressier garment for the wealthy and one less so for common folk. Even the wealthy Puritans, though, were careful not to become too fashion focused. They might use an expensive fabric—but they made it into a garment of simple style. Pride was a sin, and many ministers preached against elaborate fashion trends.

Like the Puritans, Quakers, known as the Society of Friends, also broke away from the Anglican Church of England. They believed that individuals could understand God through a personal "inner light." It was not until William Penn began his American colony of true religious freedom that they were able to practice their **pacifist** beliefs without being imprisoned.

The Quakers lived by a set of "testimonies." The testimony of simplicity included wearing plain clothing of black, brown, or gray. Men wore collarless coats and wide-brimmed hats of black or yellow. Women wore plain-cut dresses with no decoration. Their bonnets were plain cloth with stiff, deep brims. Looking at these believers was like looking inside them; their clothes reflected their hearts' desires for complete simplicity.

The Hutterites are another group who came to the New World looking for freedom. They did not swear oaths or carry weapons. Because of Canada's promise that they would not be

Modern-day Jews continue to claim both their faith and their cultural heritage with clothing for special occasions, as this boy is doing for his bar mitzvah.

forced to serve in its army, they settled there. The Hutterites used German as their language in church and read only from German sermons written in the 16th century. They hoped to keep their religion uncorrupted and pure.

For the Hutterites, living a separate life meant living together in communities. All men wore the same black clothes with simple pants, shirts, and jackets. The women wore long skirts, aprons, and headscarves. Their simple clothing helped create a feeling of togetherness for their community; it also promoted modesty and separated them from the outside world.

Using clothing to express one's spiritual beliefs may seem like a folk custom that belongs only to the past. Some modern groups, like the Hutterites, still follow this tradition.

The Amish, for example, live their lives based on this verse from the Christian New Testament: "Love not the world, neither the things

For thousands of years, people have used clothes to make religious statements. The New Testament Gospels recorded that John the Baptist wore clothes made out of camel's hair and a leather belt around his waist. This was far different from his culture's standard clothing. Those who saw him knew there was something different about him. He had separated himself from others.

that are in the world" (1 John 2:15). This Bible verse explains the Amish people's plain and simple way of life. Modest, "old-fashioned" clothes are an outward sign of their simplicity. Women's dresses are made from solid-colored fabric with long sleeves and a long full skirt. A cape and apron cover the dress. Amish women never cut their hair, and on their heads they wear a white prayer covering if they are married and a black one if they are single. Men and boys wear dark-colored suits, straight-cut coats without lapels, trousers, suspenders, solid-colored shirts, black socks and shoes, and black or straw broad-brimmed hats. Clothing colors include shades of purple, blue, wine, brown, and gray.

Religious clothing also sets apart the clergy, those who serve as ministers, priests, and nuns. The special clothing worn by

Today Amish people not only dress in a distinctive way; they also do their work and live their lives without machines, yet another statement of their faith. By refusing to adapt to the modern world, they live a life of simplicity that conforms to their religious beliefs.

those who belong to the clergy are called vestments. They originated from long-ago common clothes and have remained much the same throughout the years, even though society's fashions have changed drastically.

Priests, nuns, and pastors often wear habits or clerical collars as a sign of their faith in God. By wearing distinct clothing they enable others to recognize them as persons committed to their faith. For some **orders**, simple dress is a part of their vow of poverty. With only two or three garment changes, clothing expenses are minimal.

An alb, a long white linen robe, is worn by a Roman Catholic priest as he celebrates the Mass. This garment is like the one originally worn by residents of ancient Rome. Some of the dress for clergy evolved as a form of recognition of importance. The cassock is a floor-length robe, topped with a Roman collar. The cassock can be different colors, but the ordinary cassock is always black with various color buttons and piping for different members of the clergy.

Today, the Amish live mostly in Ohio, Pennsylvania, northern Indiana, western New York State, and Iowa. Others are located in the eastern and midwestern states and Ontario, Canada.

The liturgical clothing worn by Catholic priests has changed very little over the centuries. Modern priests still say the Mass dressed in clothing very similar to these early priests' costumes.

Like the Jews' religious clothing, the clothes of many religious orders symbolize their wearers' beliefs. The ropes tied around these monks' waists were once used for self-flagellation; the brothers beat themselves to "mortify the flesh," in an attempt to destroy their selfish natures. Today, the ropes remind their wearers to live lives of humility and sacrifice.

A nun's special clothing is called a habit. Like the word "costume," which is so closely related to the word "custom," *habit* also reminds us of custom and common practices. The word comes from a Latin word meaning "character"; just as we reveal our character with our habits or customary practices, nuns reveal their characters with their clothing, their habits.

Nuns' habits vary from one sisterhood to another. Sisters of Mary Immaculate Queen, for example, wear blue habits in honor of the Blessed Virgin, to whom the community is devoted in a special way. There have always been many different kinds and colors of sisters' habits, for there have always been many different sisterhoods within the Catholic Church, but all habits identify nuns as special servants of God.

Today, many nuns wear ordinary clothes like the rest of Western society. The original reason for habits was partly so that nuns could identify themselves with ordinary womenfolk who dressed in simple dark gowns. Over the centuries, though, women's styles have changed so radically that nuns' habits now set them apart from the rest of society. In recent years, most Roman Catholic orders have set aside their habits so that their members

The two women on the left are wearing the fashionable clothing of their day, while the woman on the right is dressed in mourning clothing. This outfit and head fashion was later used by some nuns for their habits to symbolize their identification with the world's sorrow.

Compare this nun's habit to the fashionable mourning dress in the picture above.

Widows or maidens who devoted themselves to Christian service have worn a distinct garment through-out history. Followers wanted to identify those who did charity and prayed for them so they could go to them with requests or to seek guidance.

can return to wearing the simply modest clothes worn by ordinary women.

Clearly, clothing is not only a means of displaying wealth and status; it is also an effective way to demonstrate religious devotion. Remembering who they are in relation to God and reminding others of their devotion are important to the identities of many religious people. Clothing traditions offer them one way to express themselves. Whether they choose to dress in an elaborate religious costume—or set it aside as Zuzya did—their clothes reveal their faith.

The color white has traditionally been associated with purity and sinlessness. These nuns wear white to proclaim their lifestyle to those around them.

FOUR

White as Snow,
Black as Your Hat
Clothing and Color

Stories were one way older generations passed along advice and warnings to the younger generation. This story was meant to teach young people to shun vanity and choose instead a pure lifestyle. The girl's red shoes symbolized the tempting sins of the world, while the white clothes she chooses in the end represent her salvation.

ONCE THERE WAS a pretty little girl who was very poor. She went barefoot in the summer, but for harsher weather an old shoemaker's wife made her a pair of little shoes from some old pieces of red cloth. The girl wore the beautiful red shoes for the first time to her mother's funeral. They were not appropriate for a funeral but they were all she owned.

As the girl walked to the graveyard, a carriage with an old woman came by. She was sorry for the girl and asked the clergyman if she could take care of her. At first, the girl believed this great good fortune happened to her because her red shoes were so pretty, but her benefactress burned the shoes soon after her arrival.

The time came for the girl to be *confirmed*. She would wear new white clothes and new shoes. When she and the old woman went to purchase her shoes, they found a pair of red ones. The old woman could not see very well and could not tell that they were red instead of white. She only knew that they were shiny and fit the girl well, so the old woman bought them. The girl knew her guardian would not have approved of the shoes to wear for confirmation. But she kept silent, for she longed to own another pair of red shoes.

The girl loved the red shoes so much they were all she thought of as the clergyman laid his hand upon her head and spoke of God. She could not think of anything else, only the red shoes. By the afternoon, however, the old woman heard about the girl's red shoes. She was not happy and told the girl she must wear black shoes to church from then on, even if they were old.

The next Sunday, however, the girl wore her red shoes to

Communion anyway. She and the old woman walked through a dusty path toward the church. At the door an old man asked to clean the dust off their shoes. When they were clean, everyone stared at her shoes. Once more, the girl could think of nothing but the red shoes.

After church the old man looked at the girl's shoes again and said they were such pretty dancing shoes. So the girl took a few steps for him. But once she started dancing, she could not stop. The coachman had to chase her around the church-yard and lift her into the carriage, where she kicked at the old woman until the shoes were taken off her feet. At home the shoes were put into the cupboard, but the girl could not help looking at them.

Not long after this, the girl was invited to a grand ball, so she took the red shoes out of the cupboard, delighted to have an opportunity to wear them. But at the ball, the shoes would not let her dance where she wanted, and soon she found herself out in the dark woods.

The girl danced and danced, day and night, night and day. She had no rest. As she danced past the open church door, she saw an angel in

A doctor's white clothing symbolizes sanitation and cleanliness.

We are reassured when we see that the butcher who handles our meat also wears white, indicating the sanitary conditions under which he works.

long white robes, with huge wings that touched the ground. His face was stern above his gleaming pure clothes. "Dance you shall," said he, "dance in your red shoes where proud and wicked children live, so that they may see you and fear you!"

The girl cried out to the angel. Finally, as she confessed all her sin, the angel cut the shoes off her feet and they danced away without her. At last, she was free from the wicked shoes. The next Sunday, she went to Mass dressed in purest white, and she never wore red shoes again.

THIS moralistic folktale takes pieces of European folklore and combines them with religious legends to create a tale of warning against sin. But the color white has been seen as a symbol of purity for centuries, long before the poor dancing girl was forced to give up her pretty red shoes.

White represents innocence, spotlessness, an unblemished way of life, cleanliness, and newness. Babies traditionally wear white because they've been untouched by the world. Doctors and nurses wear clean white coats as they work to help others in a sanitary and steril-

In medieval times, babies were thought to be in danger of evil spirits. Because baptism was seen as a way to keep infants pure and protected, babies wore white gowns at their baptism.

The Catholic Church's liturgical year uses color as powerful symbols. These colors are seen in the priests' vestments.

Green is the color of vegetation or life.
    It is used for Epiphany and after Pentecost.
Purple is the color of royalty.
    It is used for Advent and Lent, both seasons that celebrate the King.
White is the color of purity.
    It is the color for Easter and Christmas.
Red is the color of blood and of fire (the Holy Spirit).
    It is the color for Holy Week, Pentecost, and ordinations.

ized environment. A bride in white is a symbol of *chastity* and purity. When Roman Catholic children receive their First Holy Communion, they too dress in white dresses, pants, and shirts. These clothes are a symbol of purity; they also represent the joy of this momentous occasion.

Historically, the color white has been used to symbolize purity in many instances. In AD 325, when the Roman emperor Constantine placed Easter permanently on the calendar, he ordered everyone to wear his or her best clothing to observe the Holy Day. Because many early Christians were baptized during Easter week, white was worn to represent the cleanliness of the baptized believer and freedom from sin and guilt. This week came to be called "White Week."

Aside from Easter, *Pentecost* was the most popular day for baptisms in the church. Because of the wearing of white robes by those being baptized, Pentecost came to be known as "White Sunday."

Christians were not the only ones to connect white with pu-

A bride's white gown traditionally represents her purity and innocence.

rity. Yom Kippur is the Day of Atonement or the Day of Cleansing in the Jewish religion. The day is spent studying or praying in the synagogue. The Kol Nidre, held in the evening, before the setting of the sun, is celebrated throughout the temple with white, which symbolizes freshness and simplicity. The rabbi and the **cantor** wear white, and the Holy Ark holding the **Torah** is white also. This is a service of starting again, of newness.

That sense of new life and purity is also an important symbol for weddings. Today most wedding gowns are white, but it wasn't until 1840, when Queen Victoria wore white to marry Prince Albert, that white wedding dresses became popular.

White wedding gowns did not immediately catch on in North America. Most women in the New World could only afford to wear for their weddings a nicer version of their normal clothes, a gown that could then be worn to church or for other special occasions. Only the wealthy could afford the luxury of a white dress that would serve little practical good as a future item of clothing. With the advent of the Industrial Age, however, new machines made clothing cheaper. Fabric and clothing began to be made in factories, rather than by hand, and more and more women could afford a special white wedding gown.

Few brides dressed in white before the 19th century. In fact, according to some European traditions, white was the color of mourning. By the **Victorian** era, however, black was the color of mourning.

Black symbolized death's night and the absence of light and joy. The length of time that someone mourned depended on the individual and the person being mourned. A woman mourning her husband's death could be in deep or full mourning for six months to two years, with the traditional time being one year plus one day. During this time, the woman was expected to wear all black with no trim or jewelry unless the jewelry was *jet*. Women in deep mourning wore black from head to foot, with the exception of her undergarments. (The black dyes would have worn off on her skin). When a woman was too poor to buy a black dress, she dyed her old dresses black. Even special jewelry was designed to reflect the somber mood, and during the 19th century, mourning jewelry was often made from the deceased person's hair.

After the first year, a woman could gradually modify her mourning attire during a period of three additional stages. Second mourning lasted for about nine months; during this time, the widow was permitted to wear white collars and cuffs, and her bonnet could be lined with white. The next stage, ordinary mourning, lasted three months; during this time shiny silks and velvets were allowed. Trims of lace, ribbon, embroidery, and beading were used once more, and jewelry of gold, silver, and precious stones could now be worn again. The final stage of mourning, called half-mourning, lasted six months, and during this time sober colors like gray, mauve, purple, lavender, lilac, and white were permitted.

The practice of an outward show of inward sorrow was ob-

> Since black fabric did not wear well and turned "rusty," there were many recipes in magazines and women's books for restoring black garments.

served by nearly everyone. During World War I, however, when the United States lost 112,000 soldiers, mourning clothes restrictions began to disappear. Seeing so many women dressed in black would have been too depressing for the country as a whole.

Today white and black clothing continue to have religious and traditional significance. White has become a professional uniform for many workers that indicates cleanliness to the public. The color white reassures us that our doctors, nurses, dentists—and even our butchers—are working under sanitary conditions. Meanwhile, sober black is the proper attire for most businesspeople. Black suits have become associated with responsibility and financial power.

We seldom stop to think about what the colors of our clothes mean. But rooted in early folk traditions, white clothing continues to represent purity, new life, and cleanliness, while black conveys a heavier, more serious message. Color is yet another example of the way that clothing speaks a powerful language without ever uttering a word.

Much of North American society connects black with mourning, but this is a purely cultural connection. Other cultures dress in other colors to express their grief.

- The Chinese wear white as the color for hope.
- Persian mourning customs include brown clothing, because it is the color of withered leaves.
- Syrian mourners wear blue, because it was thought to be the color for heaven.
- In the Middle Ages, European mourners, like the Chinese, wore white to express their hope in eternal life.

For special celebrations, many people wear the ethnic costumes that reflect their wearers' cultural heritage.

FIVE

Celebrating in Style
Clothing and Fun

The clothing people wear to celebrate are often rooted in tradition and story. According to one folktale, the Chinese wear red for New Year's, because this was the color that frightened away a dangerous beast.

CELEBRATIONS ARE a way to bring people in a community or family together. These festivities often include donning special clothes. The holiday outfits indicate to ourselves and to others that this is a special time, a time set apart for celebration. Traditionally, children wear new clothes for their birthdays; we put on our best clothes for Christmas and Easter celebrations; and when we attend weddings and formal receptions, we get gussied up in our finest "duds." For other special occasions, we sometimes dress up in costumes and masks. This special clothing allows revelers to become someone else, if even for a short time.

ACCORDING to Chinese tradition, a monster beast called Nian preyed on people the night before the beginning of a new year. He had a very big mouth that would swallow a great many people with one bite. People were very scared. Finally, an old man offered to capture the beast. The man conned Nian into helping the people by challenging him to swallow other beasts more worthy to oppose him.

Nian agreed to the challenge. He swallowed many of the beasts who bothered the people. Nian was then seen riding away with the old man on his back and the people enjoyed peace. But before the old man left, he told people to wear red at each year's end to scare away Nian in case he sneaked back again. Red was the color the beast Nian had feared the most. Today, people who share a Chinese heritage still wear red for New Year's, although most have forgotten the original reason was to scare away Nian.

Although most of North America celebrates the New Year at a

At New Year's, many people dress in a variety of costumes.

different time of year from the Chinese, for many cultures, New Year's is a day of costumes and masked balls. Some of these traditions arose out of primitive cultures' belief that the New Year was a time to drive away the old and make room for the new. They wore masks to represent the spirits of the dead, and they hoped that loud noises like the beating of drums and shouting would scare away the evil spirits. If they could get rid of the wicked things of the past, they could look forward to the New Year with peace and renewal.

The Chinese New Year falls somewhere between January 21 and February 19, and the celebration lasts several days.

Some Jewish celebrations also include costume customs. Purim is a Jewish festival of rejoicing and survival, based on the biblical story of Queen Esther, a woman who saved the Jewish people from the persecution of Haman, an officer of the Persian King Ahasuerus. According to tradition, Jewish children dress up for Purim in costumes, many biblical, and go from house to house performing plays of the Purim story. They are sometimes given treats for their efforts. Adults may perform little satires of biblical characters or rabbis and even perform mock religious ceremonies.

Special clothes are a way to celebrate special days.

One New Year's Eve celebration that began with the settlers and continues today in Philadelphia, Pennsylvania, is the Mummer's Parade. It comes from the ancient English tradition of mummers, people who dressed in costumes and went from house to house, acting out plays in return for money or Christmas treats. Throughout the colonies, this tradition was a common one at Christmas time. In some regions, like the South, it was transformed into a time when neighbors went from house to house exchanging gifts of food on Christmas Day; in other places the tradition shifted to New Year's, and the focus remained on the costumes rather than the visiting. Today, the costumes worn by

Masks and funny hats help people celebrate the New Year in communities across North America.

The tradition of wearing new clothes at Easter led to the superstition that such new clothes meant the wearer would have a year of good luck. The wearing of new clothes also led to Easter parades, to show off new spring outfits after a long winter of everyday work clothes. The most famous Easter parade is held in New York City, where pets and people dress in their finest and sometimes most bizarre Easter outfits.

the mummers in the Philadelphia parade take a whole year's work because they are so elaborate.

Mardi Gras, the Tuesday before Ash Wednesday at the start of **Lent**, is another time of costumes and revelry. If you have seen the Mardi Gras celebrations of New

The costumes worn at Mardi Gras in New Orleans are often expensive and elaborate.

During the 18th century, fans were not merely a means for keeping cool. They were also important fashion accessories for women, especially at parties and other celebration. Fans had their own language.

- If the fan was moved across the cheek, the woman loved the man to whom she was speaking.
- If the woman twirled the fan in her right hand, that meant she loved someone else.

Many fans were elaborately made using gauze, silk, paper, feathers, and laces. Some had painted faces with eyes cut out that allowed the owner to watch other party guests without their knowing. Some fans were used as "cheat sheets," with dance steps, words to songs, and game rules written on the backsides to aid an absentminded woman.

Orleans, you might find it difficult to believe that all the festivities are preparation for Lent's sober season, but it is true. Since the beginning of the 18th century, Mardi Gras carnivals have been a part of New Orleans tradition. Each year, Carnival includes parades, balls, and much excitement. The members of the parade are not the only ones to dress in costume; the people in the streets also come in fancy dress. From animals to clowns to comic-strip characters, ordinary citizens take on new identities for the duration of Carnival.

Mockery is one of the high-spirited characteristics of Mardi Gras. Some costumes may allow their wearers to scoff at political or public figures they dislike. The parade gives people the opportunity to come together to promote their cause. For example, at the Mardi Gras that came during the Persian Gulf War and the one that came after September 11, 2001, many costumes were red, white, and blue, expressing their wearers' patriotism.

One of the most widespread masked celebrations in Canada and the United States is Halloween. Believed to be rooted in the Celtic festival called Samhain when evil spirits roamed the earth causing mischief, this ancient holiday includes costumes and masks. Across North America, children celebrate this festival by dressing up in different disguises. As night descends, the children visit neighbors, going door to door with cries of "Trick or treat!" Many also enjoy masquerade parties with games and good food.

A Vietnamese fall festival, Trung Thu, celebrates the beauty of the moon, but in many ways it is similar to Halloween. Vietnamese

Mardi Gras is always 47 days before Easter Sunday. The date can fall between February 3 and March 9 depending on the Catholic Church's calendar.

Mardi Gras colors are purple, green and gold, which stand for:

• Purple represents justice
• Green stands for faith
• Gold stands for power

For the Zuni Indians of New Mexico masks have a religious significance. Because rain is so scarce where they live, the Zunis pray to the rain spirits during the Shalako festival. Men of the tribe wear masks with eyes and beaks that move. Then they dance as they pretend to be rain spirits. The masks are on long poles with skirts that hide the dancer.

The Zunis prepare for this celebration all year long. The men practice the chants and dances throughout the year. If the dancers stumble or miss a step, they believe they will bring bad luck to the community.

children in North America celebrate this holiday by wearing masks, lighting lanterns, and eating special foods like moon cake. Trung Thu is also a time to remember relatives who have died.

Masks and costumes, as well as special holiday finery, are an important way for people to celebrate. Whether we are taking part in a community celebration or a private one, special clothes allow us to shed our ordinary responsibilities. They give us a new identity. For a little while we become someone else, someone who is free to laugh and have a good time.

Halloween is a time for children to dress up, taking on new identities for a night of fun.

Some work clothes are for identification—and some are for protection, as is the case with this worker.

SIX

Work Clothes
The Right Clothes for
the Right Job

The cowboy hat and cowboy boots were once considered to be work clothes. These items of clothing protected the cowboy's head and feet, making it easier for him to do his job. Today, however, they may also be fashion statements.

IF YOU WERE told there was a man in the other room who was dressed in black pants and a white dress shirt, you would not be able to tell me his occupation. But if I added that he wore a white apron and a puffy white hat, you would probably guess he was a chef—and you would be right. We could keep this guessing game going by describing someone else in a Stetson hat, a plaid shirt, denims, pointed leather boots, and fringed chaps. If you guessed cowboy, you're right again.

Many people go to work in a special uniform that identifies them with their particular job. For instance, military persons wear uniforms that help protect them as they work. Hard hats, rubber boots, gloves, and even protective eyeglasses help manual workers do their jobs. Those who manage banks, insurance companies, and other businesses dress to present a professional image and encourage a productive, competent atmosphere. Our clothes identify our work; they also serve as protection, and in many cases they make our jobs easier to do.

Early in history, most work clothes were just old clothes that were made simply and of durable materials. As a variety of fabrics became more available, most laborers chose to wear clothing that was appropriate for their jobs. Blue-collar workers, or those who do manual labor, wear rough clothing that will last well for a particular job. They want heavy fabric, like denim or canvas, for their pants and a breathable nonrestrictive fabric for shirts. Colors are dark because they show stains less. They sometimes wear a protective coverall over their other clothes to protect themselves from the dirt of their work.

For many people, work clothes are simply old clothes that won't be spoiled by the dirt of farming or other labor.

Those who work as professionals who mainly sit at a desk or do nonmanual labor today are called white-collar workers. They wear clothing that projects a certain image to the professionals and clients with whom they work. Many wear suits with ties.

The identification of blue- and white-collar workers as a description of a person's employment originated during the colonial period, but it did not become a part of our common language until the 1940s. Men's shirts, however, have distinguished their position in society for many years. Sometimes there were even laws against common people trying to imitate the dress of

APRONS

Aprons were first worn during the Middle Ages as protection for everyday clothes. During some periods aprons were embellished and were very fancy, but mostly they were just plain white. Women wore aprons to do work, both in the home and in the field, but men who worked as blacksmiths or in carpentry also wore them to protect their clothing and supply pockets for small necessities like nails, screws, and tools.

Children wore aprons called pinafores because they were "pinned afore" or on the front of their clothes. They protected clothes that were special or were not washed often.

those above them. Businessmen and men of reputation preferred their shirts snowy white.

Suit styles have changed since the 1700s. Then most men wore shirts, ties, vests, trousers, and a frock coat. Many also wore hats. Today's professional man may or may not wear a full suit—but he still dresses in styles that project an image of professional competency.

Women's work clothes have changed even more radically than men's. For centuries, European women wore dresses even for the hardest work, and they brought this tradition with them

Men's work fashions have changed over the years, but the tie, which serves no real purpose, is still a necessary accessory for proper professional attire.

A doctor's white coat reassures us that she knows how to make us feel better.

Demand for ready-made clothing led to several hundred thousand people working long hours in textile factories. Many of these workers were children. Because there were no health regulations at the time, the conditions in these mills were often unbearable. Many workers became deaf or ill from noise and fumes. Some even died.

Today few North Americans consider the fact that most of our clothing is made in other countries. Take a look at the tags inside your clothes. You'll probably find that most of them were made in various nations around the world. American clothing companies can make their products cheaper in foreign factories, partly because many of these countries have no laws against child labor or unsafe working conditions. Few of us remember that although our clothes come from factories, human hands run the machines.

to the New World. Until World War I, no woman would have dreamed of wearing pants.

But during the World Wars, the men who went to serve their country left a large gap in the work force back home. While the men were overseas fighting, many North American women had to take their places on farms and in factories. These women were doing "men's jobs," and for the first time, they wore men's clothes—trousers and overalls.

Today, judges wear long black robes, and years ago so did lawyers. For these professionals, their clothing designates authority. Policemen, firemen, and soldiers wear clothes that both protect them and indicate their authority; their uniforms allow others to recognize their expertise in a given field. For instance, if you had just witnessed a crime, you might feel great relief if you saw a police officer coming toward you. (However, if you had just run a stoplight that same officer might not be so welcome.) The next

Many years ago, one of the more interesting occupations was knighthood. These military men-at-arms wore suits of chain mail and armor. When dressed in armor, one crusader looked pretty much like any other one. So who was fighting whom? Tunics helped to identify the knight. Embellished with the colors and insignias of the ruler he served, a knight might be decorated with birds, animals, flowers, or castles. Sometimes they were identified by brightly colored tunics and robes for their horses. These colors led to some men gaining the name of the Red Knight or the Green Knight.

These men are easy to identify as "white-collar" professionals.

time you're sick and visit a doctor, when he walks in with a white jacket and stethoscope around his neck, you'll be glad to know he is a man who knows how to make you feel better.

Many people who wear uniforms conform to a specific conduct. While in uniform they pledge to be loyal and to stand for what is right. Mail carriers are committed to delivering the mail in a timely fashion, and police officers promise to protect

The World Wars changed North American clothing in more than one way. The recruits needed cloth for their uniforms, and eventually the American War Production Board regulated the use of fabric by civilians. From 1942 to 1946 a 15 percent decrease in fabric use was the goal. One way of accomplishing this was the no fabric-on-fabric rule. This meant no pleats, pockets, ruffles, trouser cuffs, or wide lapels. Skirts were shortened to the knee. Even bathing suits became smaller. The two-piece bathing suit was even considered a part of the war effort. A smaller version called a bikini was named after a U.S. military site in the South Pacific called Bikini Atoll.

Soldiers' uniforms have changed over the years, but they are still easily recognizable. This clothing makes a statement about the wearers' loyalty and commitment to a dangerous job.

those they serve. Airplane pilots and attendants take care of the passengers they transport, offering hospitality as well as expertise.

Many workers today wear uniforms to keep their street clothes clean from working conditions. Others promote an image and a product. At fast food restaurants, workers wear the colors and motifs of their company. Some manual laborers wear a jumpsuit over their regular clothes, both to protect their street clothes and to identify them as a company employee. These work clothes, like all the others we have mentioned, are yet another way that traditional fashions help us communicate who we are.

Blue jeans were once considered to be work clothes for farmers. Now they have become an ever-present part of our culture.

SEVEN

Forever in Blue Jeans
From Work Clothes to an
American Icon

Today denim is used not only for pants but for jackets and other items of clothing as well.

BEFORE THE 1940s teenagers were thought to be young adults. They went from being children straight to employment and marriage. Most of that time they dressed in miniature versions of what their parents wore. But during World War II when 18-year-olds went to war, the country suddenly noticed this important part of the population. Not long after, teen fashions became popular. One of the most important teen fashions was blue jeans.

Denim has been used to make jackets, mini-skirts, shorts, and entire outfits. It is a trendy fashion fabric that has become the popular attire for teens around the world. But denim didn't start out as a fashion fabric.

Back in 1850, Levi Straus was a young dry-goods salesman who went to California hoping to sell the gold miners tent canvas. As he watched the men work, however, he realize they had a great need for sturdy, rugged pants. He decided to make pants from the same canvas from which his tents were made. These pants would be strong and durable. His first pants were called waist overalls.

Straus opened a successful business in San Francisco. One of the changes he made to his original design was to use a fabric called serge de Nimes. Serge was a kind of fabric, and Nimes the town in France where it was made. De Nimes was later shortened to denim. Eventually denim would be made from all-cotton fabric. Straus chose to dye the fabric blue so it would show fewer stains.

Straus's partner Jacob Davis had another good idea: he added rivets to the corners of the pockets to keep them from ripping off.

Even babies wear blue jean overalls.

In 1958 jeans were displayed at the World's Fair.

In 1947, boys' jeans sold for 85 cents a pair in the Sears catalog.

Straus and Davis never suspected they were creating a style that would last for future generations. Their pants became known as Levis.

Before long, cowboys, farmers, and others who did physical labor began wearing denim. Cowboys in the 1870s wanted their Levis to fit tight because of the brush that caught at their pant legs. They could get around easier while riding horses if their pants fit close to their bodies. In order to get the tight fit they wanted, they lay in horse troughs and then let the jeans dry as they wore them.

Blue jeans are the standard clothing for most high school students.

Blue jeans are appropriate for a shopping trip . . . for school . . . for lunch with friends . . . and even sometimes for church.

Folklore stories tell of a pair of Levis being used to connect two train cars. Others tell of lives being saved from bullets deflected from rivets on Levis. Some even insist that snagged belt loops supported construction workers; men who fell from skyscraper scaffoldings claimed to have hung from a belt loop until help arrived.

In the 1930s, women first wore Levis at dude ranches that were popular places for vacationing. Children began wearing Levis for play

In 1996, over 511 million pairs of jeans were sold in the U.S.!

In 1886, Levi began sewing labels on each pair of jeans. Pictured on the label was a pair of jeans being pulled between two horses. Levis were so strong even two horses could not pull them apart.

clothes in the 1940s. But when teens began wearing jeans as their everyday clothes, denim's popularity shot sky high.

At first, most teenagers wore blue jeans called dungarees. A hit song called "Dungaree Doll" referred to the fashion craze of teenage girls wearing an untucked men's shirt over her jeans. These same girls often put on wet jeans so they dried to "fit like skin." Others used a garden hose or sat in the tub to shrink their jeans.

One **urban legend** describes the plight of a poor girl whose jeans were so tight that she had to call the fire department to help her get them off. Another tale claims that a girl wore her jeans so tight that she cut off the circulation in her legs and became para-

Although blue jeans are now fashionable, they continue to be used as work clothes as well.

Before the advent of modern cleaning, people did not wash clothes regularly. Laundering clothes took a lot of time and effort. Water was hauled from a well or stream, heated over a fire, and then clothes were scrubbed. Sweat, animal odors, fireplace smoke, and food often soiled clothes. Some spot-cleaning was done on garments but even that did not keep fleas, lice, and bedbugs from living in clothes. Aprons, caps, shirts, and shifts were laundered about once every six weeks or so.

lyzed. These stories were probably told by an older generation scandalized by their daughters' "immodest" clothing.

Jeans have remained popular for years, but movies featuring a jean-clad James Dean and motorcycle gangs dressed in jeans and leather jackets began to give denim a bad name. Some people began associating blue jeans with troublemakers and juvenile delinquents. High schools began to ban jeans as inappropriate school apparel.

By the 1960s, though, high school and college students wore jeans everywhere including rallies, music festivals, and protests. The "worn look" became the style, and new stories circulated—about burying jeans for a month or so or of sandpapering them to get them faded. There are even tales of rubbing jeans with handfuls of brick and lime dust to get that blue-white faded look.

The Smithsonian Institution keeps several pairs of blue jeans in its permanent collection. For the museum, jeans represent a part of Americana.

In 1968, Levi first began making women's jeans. Denim had become a fashion itself, with divisions for women, boys, children, and even babies.

Blue jeans are a very democratic fashion, for rich and poor alike wear them, as this author points out:

"The new clothes [jeans] express profoundly democratic values. There are no distinctions of wealth or status, no elitism; people confront one another shorn of these distinctions."
—Charles A. Reich, *The Greening of America*

For all those who bleached and shrunk, buried and rubbed, the results were a part of the phenomenon that has become an American icon. Denim pants that started as the necessary clothes of gold diggers have become the everyday dress of rich and poor, male and female, and young and old. Jeans are always in style.

What are you doing today? Just throw on a pair of jeans and a shirt, and you're dressed appropriately for just about anything.

Jeans are named after cloth originally made in Genoa, Italy and then manufactured in France. The French called the cloth Genes, which is the French name for Genoa.

One of the good things about jeans is that they do not have to be laundered as often as other fabric. Did you ever wonder how long you could wear a pair of jeans without washing them? There are numerous urban legends circulating about who could keep a pair of jeans on the longest. Someone claimed to have kept the same pair on for eight months, even while he bathed and slept.

Today we all have many fashion options; each one reveals a different personality type, or different aspects of the same personality. Judging from this man's clothes, how would you describe his personality?

EIGHT

Changing Fashions
The Meaning of Clothing Today

Like the little old lady in this story, we all depend on clothes to give us a sense of who we are.

ONCE THERE WAS a little old lady who lived all alone in the country. Some days she hankered for the company of others; she got tired of hearing only her own voice. In fact, some days she wondered if she existed at all, living all by herself the way she did.

So one day, she decided to fancy herself up in her best clothes and head to town. First, she put on her petticoat with the four ruffles. Then she slipped into her favorite blue dress with the shiny buttons and the lace trim. Last of all, she put on her fine leather shoes with the buckles. When she looked down at herself, she was very pleased with the person she saw. She no longer wondered if she existed, for her beautiful clothes told her she was a fine woman indeed. She set off happily for town.

But along the way, the little old lady got tired. "I will just sit down here by the side of the road and rest my bones a moment," she said to herself. She leaned back against a tree and cast one last look down at the fine blue dress with the shiny buttons. She could see her best petticoat peeping out beneath the hem, and she smiled at her stout leather shoes with the buckles. "What a good person they will think me when I reach town," she said and closed her eyes.

The little old lady fell sound asleep. She slept so deeply that she did not hear when a robber came walking along the road to town and stopped beside her. His long shadow fell across her as she slept, but she never knew.

The robber looked at the little old lady's nice blue dress with the shiny buttons and the lace trim. He smiled at her fine leather

shoes with their bright buckles. And then carefully, carefully, oh so carefully so as not wake her, he took a sharp bright knife from his pocket and bent over the little old lady.

Whisk! He cut off her shiny buttons, all eight of them, and popped them into his pocket. Whit-whit-whit! He slashed off the fancy lace trim and wound it into a ball. Whish-whish! His sharp bright knife trimmed the ruffles off her best petticoat. He folded them up neatly and put the lace and the ruffles in his pack. Then he bent down on one knee and slipped her fine leather shoes with the bright shiny buckles right off her feet. In his pack they went. And then the robber continued on his way, whistling to himself. He knew he would get a tidy sum in town for his new goods.

A fly landed on the little old lady's nose and woke her. She stretched and opened her eyes. Her gaze fell on her ragged dress and stockinged feet, and she began to cry. "Alas! Alack! I went to sleep a fine lady—but this is none of me! This is none of me!"

She was too ashamed to continue on to town. Instead, she stumbled home in her stocking feet, still sobbing, "This is none of me!"

As the old lady in this Appalachian folktale discovered, clothes are important to our sense of

Wearing emblems on clothes has become extremely prevalent in the United States and Canada. Men, women, and children wear the logos of teams, NASCAR drivers, manufacturers, and more on their hats, jackets, and sports clothes. By doing so, they identify themselves with a particular group or try to impress others by their clothing choices.

identity. They are one way we identify ourselves to the world around us. They give us a sense of who we are. They may make us feel important, attractive, grown up, professional, or imposing.

In the past, many people drew their sense of who they were from their cultural community. Different groups were identified by locality, and their clothes reflected these regional identities. When first moving to North America, immigrants from individual countries or communities settled near each other so they shared common foods, beliefs, customs—and clothing traditions.

Today, however, we are less apt to dress in a way that identifies us with our ethnic heritage, and more apt to wear clothes that indicate our jobs or even our religious beliefs. Celebrations give us opportunities to identify ourselves in different ways from what we would do ordinarily.

Contemporary North Americans have a variety of reasons for choosing their clothes. Many people today select their clothing because of designer tags or to identify themselves with sports figures or celebrities, and more. Street gangs wear a certain style of clothing that identifies them; sports teams wear distinctive uniforms, and their fans may also wear clothing with the same logos or design. Anyone who follows a special team knows their colors and their emblem and usually owns numerous garments advertising them.

Until very recently, there have always been clothing differences between the sexes. Men and women went out of their way to look different from one another. Many times, married women dressed differently than single women. Even if the difference was only slight, a woman's marital status was defined by her clothing. Today all that has changed. Women continue to wear dresses for formal occasions, but more and more women dress in blue jeans or other pants for their everyday attire. Men's clothing and women's clothing are very similar.

The clothing worn by these young men is also a cultural statement. Their clothing gives them a sense of belonging to a group; it proclaims their identity to the world.

Sports clothing has also become an important part of many people's wardrobe, whether or not they are athletes. Sweat pants, sweatshirts, and leotards are all standard casual wear today, even if the wearer has no intention of working up a sweat. Much of sports clothing is embroidered or embellished with sayings, cartoons, or symbols. T-shirts are an important part of this clothing style.

These shirts are not new to our generation, however. Initially they were worn as undergarments during World War I by enlisted men. The popularity of the T-shirt gained importance when male actors first wore them without other shirts covering them. By the 1950s, they had become an important part of teen fashion. During the 1970s, printed T-shirts became a way for music groups and sports teams to make money and advertise at the same time.

For most people, but perhaps especially for teenagers, clothing is an important and endlessly fascinating part of their lives. But all of us need to remember that we are more than our clothing. The little old lady in the story was wrong: our identities will not disappear if our fancy clothing is removed.

This point is illustrated by a Jewish folktale about a rich man

In today's fitness-conscious world, sports clothes are acceptable both for exercise and for casual wear.

CLOTHING FASTENERS

How we fasten our clothing has changed over the years—and like everything else about our clothes, some fasteners have a deeper significance. For instance, some religious groups, like the Amish, use only pins as fasteners; they believe that buttons might lead to vanity. Priests' cassocks have 33 buttons, representing Christ's earthly years.

Other fasteners we take for granted today are relatively new on the scene. The zipper, for example, was patented on August 29, 1893 by a mechanical engineer—but his design had a big problem: it didn't work. Not only did it not work, but no one wanted it. At the Chicago World's Fair the inventor only managed to sell 20 zippers, all to the U.S. Postal Service to close their mailbags. In 1913, a better model was produced, but it too had a drawback: it rusted closed after washing. World War II was going on, and the U.S. Army decided to try the zipper for clothing and equipment. But the zipper didn't catch on with the general public. Believe it or not, people couldn't figure out how to use it. (It actually came with directions.) Finally, in 1923, B.F. Goodrich ordered 150,000 of the new fasteners for *his* new product: rubber galoshes. Goodrich also coined the term zipper.

In 1948, a new fastener came on the scene. A Swiss mountaineer named George de Mestral was frustrated by the burs that clung to his clothes when he was walking through the woods. As he picked them off, however, he realized he could use the bur's basic structure to make a fastener to compete with the zipper. He liked the sound of "vel" from velvet and "cro" from the French word crochet (meaning hook)—Velcro®. By the end of the 1950s, 60 million yards of the fastener was being produced each year.

who had grown ill. He went from doctor to doctor, but no one could find a cure. One day the man heard about a young doctor who was visiting a nearby town, so he went to see him.

After a thorough examination the doctor told the man he knew of a cure for his illness. The man was pleased and waited to hear the doctor's recommendation.

"Find the shirt of a man without worries," the young doctor told him.

The rich man hired two servants to search for a man without worries and to bring back his shirt. From place to place the men traveled seeking the shirt and the man who wore it. But they could not find anyone who had no worries.

The servants were just about to go back and report their failure to the rich man, when they met an extremely cheerful and friendly gentleman sitting beside a little house. They went up to the man and questioned him for some time.

Apparently, they had found what they were seeking: the man did not have any worries. He assured them that there was nothing worrying him at all.

"Why should I worry," the man told the servants. "See that lake. It is full of fish and those fields grow abundant crops. I feel very secure."

"Well," said the other servant. "We are very happy to have met you. But we are looking for something that we would like to purchase from you. We will pay you very well for it."

"I don't have anything to sell to you," the man said.

"We just wish to buy your shirt," one servant said.

The man began to laugh. "Like I said, I don't have anything to sell you. I don't wear a shirt at all."

The surprised servants left without the cure. They felt very gloomy to have to return to the rich man unsuccessfully. When they arrived home they told him they had indeed found a man without worries—but when asked for the shirt, they had to admit their failure.

"Why is this?" the rich man asked.

"Well," one servant said, "the man did not own a shirt."

Of all the things you wear, your expression is the most important.
—Janet Lane

Bathing suits reflect the moral issues of the times. Up until the 1920s, women wore some form of the bloomer. Early styles consisted of a full-length bloomer and a top or tunic with long sleeves. A woman's body had to be covered at all times. But bathing suits became shorter and shorter, both sleeves and pant legs, until by the 1930s one-piece suits were short and very revealing. Suits were usually made of cotton and sometimes wool. Men's suits were also one piece. In 1946 the first bikini appeared. Although they were not the string bikinis of the 1970s, baring a woman's midriff, arms, legs, and neck was a big change.

"So the man without any worries did not have a shirt at all." The rich man scratched his chin. "Now I know what I have to do to get well." He thanked the men and paid them for their services.

From then on, the rich man began to give away his money to other people until finally he no longer had any worries himself.

THE sick man in this folktale understood something that the little old lady failed to grasp: some things are more important than our clothes.

Clothing can be creative expressions of identity. Our garments can communicate something about us without us ever saying a word. Clothes can give us a feeling of belonging, a sense that we "fit in." But clothing is only a material possession—and ultimately too many possessions can load us down with worries. What was meant to affirm our identities can actually rob us of what is truest and best about ourselves.

The answer may be simply to choose your clothing consciously, rather than allowing some outside force to do all the dictating. We can choose to wear what is appropriate for a given situation without becoming "slaves to fashion."

Don't be like the foolish emperor, who allowed himself to be so swayed by his vanity that he made a silly choice of wardrobe. The next time you get dressed, think about it. Why do you wear the clothes you do? What are they communicating about you?

What do you want to communicate?

Further Reading

Ewing, Elizabeth. *Everyday Dress 1650–1900*. New York: Chelsea House Publishers, 1984.

Davis, Fred. *Fashion Culture and Identity*. Chicago: University of Chicago Press, 1992.

Joseph, Nathan. *Uniforms and Non-Uniforms: Communication Through Clothing*. New York: Greenwood, 1986.

Miller, Brandon Marie. *Dressed for the Occasion*. Minneapolis, Minn.: Lerner Publications Company, 1999.

Perl, Lila. *From Top Hats to Baseball Caps, From Bustles to Blue Jeans*. New York: Clarion Books, 1990.

Tuleja, Tad. *Curious Customs*. New York: Harmony Books, 1987.

For More Information

Costume Page
members.aol.com

Folk Costume
virtual.park.uga.edu/~clandum/category_html/costume.html

Polish Folk Costumes
www.chebucto.ns.ca

Victorian Women's Fashions
victoriana.com

Zippers and Velcro®
mmbers.tripod.com/~earthdude1/zippers/zippers.html

Glossary

Aesthetically Appealing to the sense of beauty.

Cantor A Jewish official who sings or chants the music and leads the congregation in prayer.

Challis A lightweight soft fabric made from cotton or wool.

Chastity Purity; a state of refraining from sexual activity before marriage.

Confirmed Participated in the Christian rite whereby a young person becomes a full member of the church and thereby "confirms" his or her faith.

Distaff A staff for holding the unspun fiber during spinning.

Hemp A tough plant fiber used for making rope.

Indigenous Occurring naturally in a particular environment or region.

Jet A polished stone from very hard coal used for jewelry.

Magistrates A legal official.

Motifs A recurring design.

Orders Religious communities.

Pacifist A person who is morally against using violence, even in war.

Pentecost The church holy day that commemorates the Holy Spirit's coming.

Sects Religious groups.

Synagogue A Jewish place of worship.

Torah Jewish Scripture.

Urban legend A contemporary folktale that circulates through modern society.

Victorian Having to do with the period when Queen Victoria ruled England in the 19th century.

Index

Biographies

Sherry Bonnice lives in a log cabin on a dirt road in Montrose, Pennsylvania, with her husband, teenage daughter, five dogs, and 25 rabbits. She loves homeschooling her daughter, reading, and making quilts. Sherry has spent the last two years coediting three quilt magazines and writing a quilt book. Writing books for children and young people has been her dream.

Dr. Alan Jabbour is a folklorist who served as the founding director of the American Folklife Center at the Library of Congress from 1976 to 1999. Previously, he began the grant-giving program in folk arts at the National Endowment for the Arts (1974–76). A native of Jacksonville, Florida, he was trained at the University of Miami (B.A.) and Duke University (M.A., Ph.D.). A violinist from childhood on, he documented oldtime fiddling in the Upper South in the 1960s and 1970s. A specialist in instrumental folk music, he is known as a fiddler himself, an art he acquired directly from elderly fiddlers in North Carolina, Virginia, and West Virginia. He has taught folklore and folk music at UCLA and the University of Maryland and has published widely in the field.